To Victor

Production and copyright © 1992 Rainbow Grafics International—
Baronian Books SC, Brussels, Belgium.
English translation text copyright © 1993 by Lothrop, Lee & Shepard Books.
All rights reserved. No part of this book may be reproduced or utilized in any form
or by any means, electronic or mechanical, including photocopying and recording,
or by any information storage and retrieval system, without permission in writing
from the Publisher. Inquiries should be addressed to Lothrop, Lee & Shepard Books,
a division of William Morrow & Company, Inc., 1350 Avenue of the Americas,
New York, New York 10019. Printed in Belgium. Printed in EEC.

First Edition   1 2 3 4 5 6 7 8 9 10

Library of Congress Cataloging in Publication data was not available in time
for publication of this book, but can be obtained from the Library of Congress.
ISBN 0-688-12375-9   Library of Congress Catalog Card Number: 92-54430

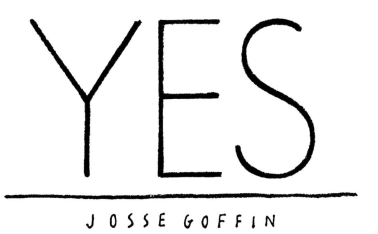

YES

JOSSE GOFFIN

Lothrop, Lee & Shepard Books
New York

No